AMAZING ESME

and the Pirate Circus

★ ★ ★ ★ ★ ★ ★ ★ ★ ★ ★ ★

Tamara Macfarla.

ILLUSTRATED BY

Michael Fowkes

Hodder
Children's
Books

A division of Hachette Children's Books

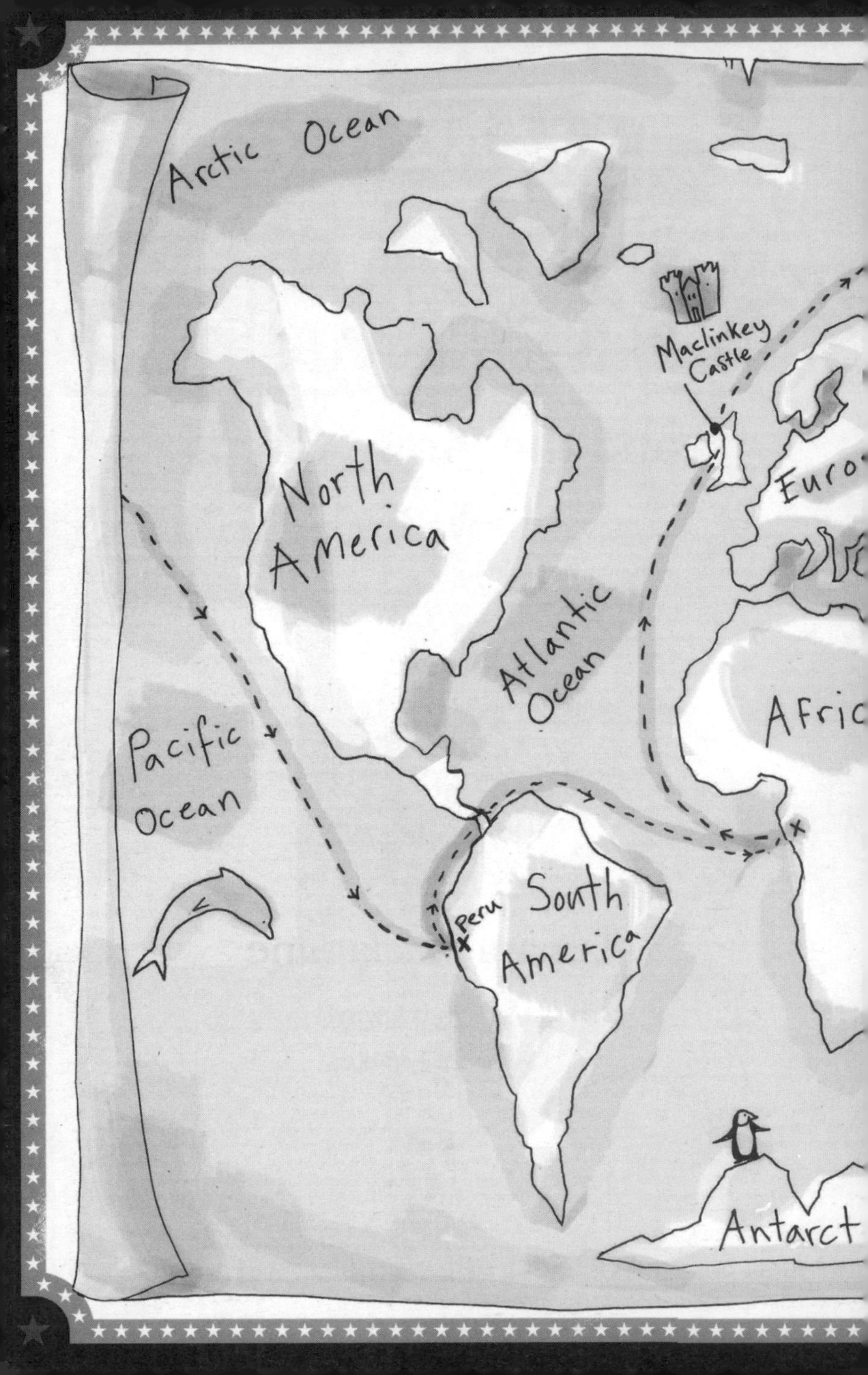
Arctic Ocean
Maclinkey Castle
North America
Atlantic Ocean
Euro
Afric
Pacific Ocean
South America
Peru
Antarct

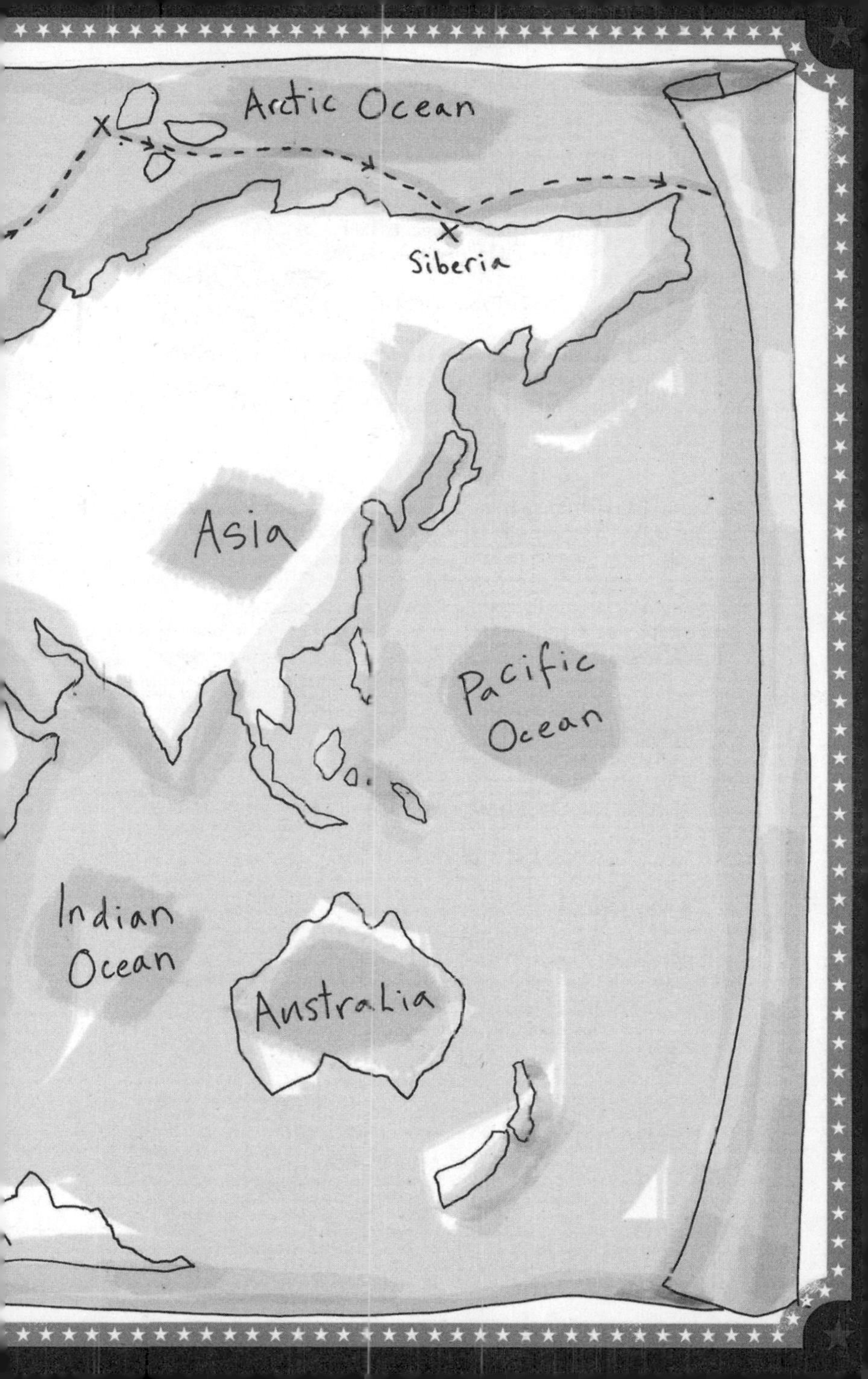
Arctic Ocean
Siberia
Asia
Pacific Ocean
Indian Ocean
Australia

For the amazing Lillie McCotter

Contents

★ ★ ★

★ ★ ★

Spooks and Spiders

'Oh, you've finally decided to turn up,'
grumbled Cosmo as Esme bounced into the
room. 'What took you so long?'

Thinking about her three-day journey up
from the circus, first by caravan and tractor,
then by boat and finally by postal van, Esme
decided it would take too long to even begin
to explain.

'Why? What am I late for?' she replied,
surprised by Cosmo's question. Meals were

the only thing that ever ran on time at Maclinkey castle and she was fairly sure that it was still a little too early for supper and quite a lot too late for lunch.

'Our Halloween party, of course,' Cosmo said. 'I can see you haven't changed since the summer. You still don't know anything.'

'Cosmo!' Magnus called warningly. 'Stop being rude to Esme. Hi, Esme. How long are you staying for?' Magnus smiled, happy to see her.

'My parents are coming up for Christmas,' Esme replied. 'They said they'd collect me in about four months when Circus Miranda has finished its round the world tour.'

'Sit down, Esme,' ordered Cosmo, picking

up a book. 'I was telling a ghost story before you rudely interrupted.'

Esme put down her suitcase, unwrapped Gus, who had hurled himself at her, stepped over a pygmy hippo, around a sloth and reached over to stroke the tall proud head of the Arctic tiger they had rescued last summer.

'You're looking so much better,' Esme said, admiring the tiger's glossy coat while he purred at her. She sat down and leant back on Donk who had turned himself into a large floor cushion.

'It was a dark . . . and stormy . . . night—' Cosmo paused to check that they were all listening. 'It was a dark and stormy night . . .' he repeated slowly, in a deep and scary voice. 'And the captain said to his crew . . .'

Gus pulled Donk's
ears down to cover
his own. 'Stop, stop,
stop! It's too scary. I
can't listen anymore,'
he squeaked.

'Don't be
ridonkulous,' Cosmo yelled.
'I've hardly even started yet!'

He began again, 'It was a dark and
stormy night and the captain said to his crew,
"Tonight, me lads, if those scavenging pirates
don't take us down to rest beneath the sea,
we'll be back safe upon home shores." And
he counted his sailors, twenty seven in all,
and steered the boat for home.'

'I'm really, really scared.' Gus peeped out

from between Donk's ears.

'Nothing scary has even happened yet!' Cosmo shouted back.

Magnus patted the cushion between him and Esme. 'Gus, come and sit with us.'

'Oh I give up. I'm not reading any more. I'm bored.' Cosmo put down the book of ghost stories, folded his arms and waited for everyone to beg for him to start again.

Esme looked up eagerly. 'Please read it, Cosmo. I've never been to a Halloween party before and I don't know any ghost stories, except circus ones. I really want to hear it.'

Cosmo poked at the fire. 'Nope, I'm not reading it.'

'Just get on with it or you'll spoil the ghost evening,' Magnus said. 'You know you want to.' He glanced over at the table behind them where a spooky feast had quietly appeared. A tail was disappearing beneath it.

'Fine then. But this is the last time.' Cosmo picked up the book. 'It was a . . .'

'No. No. No. No. No. Not from the beginning again,' Magnus pleaded.

'Hmmmph,' huffed Cosmo loudly. '"The rain hurtled down and lashed the decks and the wind whistled a dangerous tune in the sailors' ears . . ."'

'What was the tune?' Gus asked. 'Can you sing it for me?'

'Guuuuusssssssss!' Cosmo shouted. 'Get out! Go! And don't come back! You are the most annoying thing on Annoying Road, in Annoying Town in the country of Annoying in a really annoying world. I can't take any more of you. Now go.' He pointed to the stairs. 'Don't come back!'

Gus huddled back down between Magnus and Esme. 'Don't make me go. I'll be quiet. I promise. I just wanted to know how it sounded.'

Gus put his small hand into Esme's. She squeezed it reassuringly.

'Hurry up, Cosmo, but please not from the beginning again.' Magnus's stomach was beginning to call for food.

Cosmo read on. 'So the waves rose up to warn them. They flung themselves at the sides of the boat and hammered on the hull. But the sailors had caught a glimpse of home and their eyes could only look forwards.'

'Behind them, a nightmare rose from the tantruming ocean. A ghostly galleon sawed through the surface of the sea. A huge hulking skeleton of a pirate ship with a mast and boom shaped like bones. It loomed like a violent storm above them . . .'

'I need cake, I need cake, I need cake,' Gus yelled, running away from the story.

'That's it! THE END!' Cosmo called, running after him. 'Last one to the table's a donkey.'

'But I actually want to hear the end,' Esme said. 'What happens to them? Do the pirates get them? Do they get home?'

'Who cares?' Cosmo said through a mouthful of blood-and-brains raspberry muffins. 'There's food.'

Before the boys could clear every single plate of meringue and cream eyeballs, blood red jellies, liquorice cobwebs with chocolate spiders, hamburger bats, sausage slugs and marshmallow toadstools, Esme dived in.

Peering over her huge mound of food, she grinned at her cousins. Magnus, Cosmo and Gus turned to grin back at her.

Then they froze.

ONE
★ ★ ★

Tips and Tricks

'What?' whispered Esme, not daring to glance over her shoulder.

'The cups on the dresser, they're . . . moving,' Magnus said, very slowly. His eyes fixed on the tall cupboard behind Esme.

'They can't be,' she said. 'That's impossible.'

'I know,' said Cosmo, clinging on tightly to the Arctic tiger's mane. 'But they are.'

'Oh, stop teasing, Cos. It's just another

one of your tricks,' said Esme. 'I'm not falling for it this time.'

'It's not a trick, Es. Honestly, I saw them move too,' Magnus said.

'And me,' squeaked Gus from under the table.

Esme edged her way sideways towards Donk. 'But it's fine now, isn't it?' she said uncertainly. 'It's stopped. Probably just a gust of wind or something. Nothing to worry about.'

A booming ghostly voice came from somewhere around them. 'AYE AYE ME HEARTIES . . . TAKE YOU DOWN BENEATH THE WAVES . . . WAAAAAYYYYYYY DOWN . . . ' A loud clattering started on the dresser. Cups and jugs were swinging from side to side. Teapots tipped and lids chattered.

'Aaaaaaaaaaaaaaaaaaaaaaaaaaaaaaaaaaa rrrrrrrrrggggggggghhhhhhhhh . . . *run for ittttttttttttttttt!*' yelled Cosmo.

After a bit of hunting, Mrs Larder found them huddled together under the desk in the library, too scared to speak.

'Oh, that was so much fun.' She laughed as she brought them back down to finish their Halloween supper. 'Oh, I haven't laughed so much in ages.' She chuckled again, wiping away the tears. 'Oh, the look on all of your wee faces!' She stopped to hold her sides for a moment. 'I only wish I could get you to move that fast when jobs need doing.'

'But how did you do it, Mrs Larder?' asked Esme. 'How did you get the cups to move? You weren't even in the room!'

'And why, Lardie?' Gus looked at her with wide, hurt eyes. 'Why would you want to scare us?'

'Oh ducks, I love you all to the bottom of the deepest ocean and back,' said their housekeeper, 'but it *is* Halloween.' Mrs Larder wrapped her large arms around Gus and pulled him onto her lap.

'Please tell us how you did it, Mrs Larder,' Esme asked again.

Mrs Larder reached for a meringue eyeball. 'Och, it was an old trick that my mother taught me when we had visitors who wouldn't leave.' She chewed thoughtfully and chuckled at the memory. 'We tied fine white cotton thread around the handles of all the things on the dresser

in one long thread and then took the
end outside the window.' She paused for
another mouthful. 'Just when they were
least expecting it we would pull on the
thread and everything would rattle. They
never stayed long after that.'

By now Uncle Mac had come down to
join them and he laughed along from his
chair by the fire.

'I played the same trick on your fathers
when they were boys. It took me a whole day
to get them to come out from under their
bed covers, they were so scared.' Mrs Larder
began to laugh her soft rumbling laugh again.

'Now Mrs Larder, I'm sure that they've
heard quite enough,' said Uncle Mac, leaning
forwards. 'Esme's father and I weren't really
scared, we were just playing along.'

Mrs Larder winked at them all.

'Children, I need to talk to you,' Uncle
Mac sounded serious. 'Finish your mouthfuls
and come and sit by the fire.'

Magnus wandered over while Esme,
Cosmo and Gus stuffed as much food in their

mouths as they could. They grabbed at every last morsel while the table was cleared by Mrs Larder and her troop of kitchen-trained guinea pigs.

Uncle Mac began. 'I am preparing to leave on a long and important trip next week. The animals you rescued from the pirate circus last summer are now healthy enough to be returned.' He reached out an arm, scooped up the pygmy hippo and held him up in one hand for them to see. 'Well done, Magnus. Excellent work. Just look at the healthy shine in Bob's eyes.'

Bob the pygmy hippo smiled a little more brightly and opened his eyes a little wider so that they could all admire him. Magnus looked down modestly and smiled to himself with pride. They had arrived hungry and with terrible injuries from the pirate circus. He had worked hard to nurse them all back to health.

'Anyway,' Uncle Mac continued, 'I will be gone until Christmas so I need you all to be on your best behaviour and to help Mrs Larder.'

'But why now?' asked Cosmo. His father had been home for a whole month this time. Cosmo didn't want him to go.

'I am concerned that the pirate circus will come after the animals. They were furious when the inspector took them. It is not safe for Bob, Saskia and Sid here. They will be happier in the wild, where they belong.'

'Which animal will you take home first?' asked Magnus, realizing how much he was going to miss them.

Uncle Mac unrolled a large map and spread the world out in front of them.

He put Bob down and picked up the sloth's arm to use as a pointer. 'Freddie the Narwhal needs returning to his pod about here.'

'From there I'll sail on to Siberia to drop Saskia the Siberian tiger back home.

'Then down to South America to deliver Sid, here,' he said, waving Sid the sloth's arm at them. Sid snored gently.

'And finally cutting through the Panama Canal to Africa to drop Bob back.' Uncle Mac finished with a flourish of the sloth's arm.

'Any questions?' he asked, looking up at Esme and his sons.

'Can I come with you?' Magnus asked quietly.

'Well, if he's going. I'm coming,' said Cosmo. Loudly.

'Don't take me. Don't make me go. I'm not going,' said Gus. 'Just think about all the pirates.'

'Why would you want to come with me?' Uncle Mac asked Magnus in surprise. '*The Golden Gumball* is not a very big boat.'

'I need to see the animals go safely back to their families,' Magnus said. 'They'll be scared. I need to be there to let them know that they'll be safe.' He looked his father in the eye. 'They trust me.'

'You do have a point,' said Uncle Mac seriously. 'I will think about it.' He sat back in his armchair and stroked his beard. 'Right,' he said, less than a minute later. 'I've thought about it. No. It's not a good idea.'

'And why not?' asked Cosmo

'Well, for one thing, Mrs Larder,' replied Uncle Mac. 'What on earth would she do without you all here to look after?'

'All the jobs that I haven't had time to do for the last thirteen years, I should think,' muttered Mrs Larder as she staggered past with an armful of plates topped with two feathered iguanas.

TWO

★ ★ ★

Midnight
Meetings

'Wake up, Donk!' Esme stood on her bed
in her turret top bedroom and shook him
gently. 'Magnus is flashing his torch at the
window. We have to go and see what he
needs.'

She dragged a half-asleep Donk onto the
floor and stepped on him to push open the
window. Hopping out to the windowsill, she
leant down and pulled his hooves up.

'Wake up, Donk!' she said more sternly.

'Jump out of the window, now!'

Esme dropped down on to the high wire running between her turret and Magnus's and tiptoed across in her pyjamas. Donk plodded after her.

Magnus leant out of the window to meet them. 'Thanks for coming over.'

Hanging upside down, Esme's face was

level with his. 'What is it, Mags? Is one of the animals sick?' she asked.

'No,' said Magnus. 'I need your help to think of a plan. I have to get Dad to take me with him.'

'What's all the noise about?' called Cosmo, opening his window on another turret.

Esme answered in a loud stage whisper. 'Shh. Magnus needs our help to go on the trip.'

'I've already said, if he's going, I'm going,' Cosmo shouted back.

'Not me,' called Gus from the last turret. 'I'm not going to sea. See you at the top of Mags's turret, Cosmo. Three, two, one, race you . . .'

'OK. Let's find a way for Dad to take all of us then,' Magnus said.

'But not me,' said Gus, panting from the run to the top of the turret.

'Yes and you,' said Magnus. 'Bob will want you there. You're his favourite.'

'But the pirates . . . ' started Gus.

'Close your beak, Gus,' Cosmo ordered.

'There are no real pirates. It was just a story.'

'The problem is Mrs Larder,' said Magnus. 'Dad thinks she'll get lonely, even though we know she won't.'

'What if Mrs Larder has to go away? Then we can all go,' said Esme, walking along the high wire on her hands. 'Last summer she had to look after her great aunt. That's why you came to stay with me. What if her great aunt needed her again? Perhaps we could find her and ask her.'

'Or, it would be quicker if we just sent a letter to Mrs Larder pretending to *be* the great aunt?' said Cosmo.

'But isn't that sort of lying?' asked Esme.

Cosmo thought for a moment. 'Not if the aunt actually needs help,' he said. 'Which she obviously does because she's at least a hundred and forty-two.'

'It might be the only way,' said Magnus.

'In fact, then we're actually helping the elderly. Which is a good thing. Now, stop causing problems and help me write the letter. It has to be in old people speak. Esme, grab me a pen and some paper,' Cosmo ordered.

Esme flipped upside down on the wire and reached in through Magnus's window.

Cosmo started to write …

Dearest Darling Lavinia,
I am most terribly, frightfully, horrendously sorry to trouble you, My one and only relative <u>in the World</u> and my favourite niece, but I find that I am not quite managing to get around very much these days

'Hold on!' said Esme. 'What if she's already died? Mrs Larder will absolutely know that we made it up and we'll never be allowed to go to sea.'

'If she had died,' replied Cosmo impatiently, 'there would have been a funeral and we would have been made to go and look sad even though we didn't know her just like we did with that scary old man up the road three years ago. Anyone remember a funeral for a great aunt? No. Good. Now stop interrupting and think old people's thoughts so the letter sounds right.'

Cosmo continued . . .

It has been weeks now since I have been able to prepare a meal

'You can't write that,' said Magnus. 'She would have starved to death if she hadn't eaten for weeks. Then we definitely would be going to her funeral.'

Esme continued . . .

It has been quite some days now since I have been able to make my poor weak legs strong enough to carry me into the kitchen and I do so worry about falling asleep whilst cooking my tea and ending up with my frightfully, lovely flowery violet cardigan on fire ☹

'That's good, Esme,' said Magnus. 'It makes it sound more like an emergency. Mrs

Larder will definitely go and save her.'

please please please
come quickly. I am so
weak that I can barely
finish this letter

'Yes. Perfect!' said Esme.

'I'll make the writing go even more
spidery and wobbly in that bit so it looks
as though she can hardly hold the pen any
longer,' said Cosmo. He wrote . . .

With fondest Love,
your devoted aunt
who Looked after you as
a child when no one else
Wanted you — x xX

'What was the aunt called?' asked Magnus.
'She wouldn't sign it "Great Aunt", would she?'

Esme thought hard. 'I think that it might be Mildew or Milberry or Mouldeera, or maybe Limily, but I can't quite remember.'

'Maybe I'll just write it in a really scratchy way as though she dropped the pen halfway through and was too weak to pick it up,' Cosmo suggested, putting a final unreadable scratch to the page and folding the paper over.

'Right, everyone lick the envelope for good luck,' Magnus said, passing it around.

Cosmo handed him the letter. 'Gus, as soon as the sun comes up tomorrow morning, ride one of the animals to the end of the drive and ask the postman to deliver this. Just pretend it's one of your silly games.'

'I really hope this works,' said Magnus, stroking Saskia who had prowled up to be closer to him.

THREE

★ ★ ★

Trouble

'She's opening the letter now,' Magnus said, sticking his head out. 'Stay under there until we see what happens.'

They shuffled for space beneath a shaggy Highland cow. Each of them tried to shove the others out of the way to peer out as Mrs Larder read the letter. When she'd finished, she walked back into the castle, shaking her head. They all held their breath when Uncle Mac appeared in the doorway not long afterwards.

'Magnus, Cosmo, Gus and Esme!' he shouted crossly. 'Where *are* you? I need you here. Right now.'

'We're in trouble,' said Cosmo, 'I told you the letter was a bad idea.'

'No you didn't,' said Magnus. 'It was your idea.'

'Wasn't!' said Cosmo.

Uncle Mac hollered. 'If you don't come here right now, there will be no breakfast.'

'We'd better go,' said Magnus. 'If he's threatening our food he must be furious.'

'If we get close and his eyes have turned purple,' Cosmo whispered to Esme as they walked slowly towards the castle, 'run away as fast as you can.'

Donk squealed as Esme squeezed him

out of nervousness.

'Is everything OK, Dad?' Magnus asked
innocently

'No. Mrs Larder's aunt is ill. AGAIN!'
said Uncle Mac. 'You have to go and pack.
As though I don't have enough to do …'
he muttered through the hallway, throwing
ropes and maps and compasses into a large
canvas bag.

The children walked in single file behind him waiting to hear what was going to happen to them while she was gone. Hoping, but not daring to ask.

'Pack plenty of jumpers. The Arctic will be freezing,' he stated, slightly unnecessarily. 'And a swimming costume,' he added. 'The equator will be boiling.'

He threw in a torch and three huge jackets and a pair of gloves. 'Actually, pack everything that you own. Who knows what children need on a round the world expedition? I am quite sure that nobody has ever been mad enough to take one child with them before, never mind four.'

Gus sulked while Esme, Magnus and Cosmo threw their arms in the air and danced a silent dance of delight behind their father's back. Then they ran to pack.

This didn't take long. The boys managed to fit everything in one old trunk between them. Cosmo threw the pirate ghost book in on top and closed the lid.

After inspecting the trunk, Mrs Larder took everything out again and re-packed it

for them. Magnus had only packed books.
Cosmo had packed nothing except a packet
of biscuits, the pirate book and a large carrot
cake. Gus had a jar of minnows, a packet of
felt tips, some coloured paper and a couple
of puffball penguins.

'There now!' Mrs Larder sighed fondly
as she did up the buckles. 'At least there are
clean pants and warm jumpers.'

'I'll be away for my birthday.' Gus tucked
himself under Mrs Larder's arm and tried not
to cry.

Back in her room, Esme threw open
the wardrobe doors. She gathered up all of
the things that she had emptied out of her
suitcase the day before, then she tipped them
back in again. She pushed the battered case

out of the window, leapt on top of it and slid down the turret slide, whooping as she whipped around the corners and flew out over the moat.

Donk slid down behind her, using his hooves as brakes. He stepped off the end of the slide and walked over to join the gathering group of bags, animals and people, ready to load up the boat and set sail.

FOUR
★ ★ ★

Sails, Whales
and High Seas

'You're sure there's
no such thing as
ghost pirates, aren't
you?' asked Gus. Again.
He put Bob on the back of a
homemade skateboard and wheeled
him up the planks.

'I'm sure I've told you not to talk,' said
Cosmo meanly, heaving Sid down from his
back and onto the deck.

Magnus walked alongside Saskia with his hand resting on her head.

'Freddie's fed and ready for the long swim,' Esme called from the far side of the boat where she was checking on the Narwhal. She breathed in the sea and the smell of fresh paint from the boat.

'Good. Now, we can explore the *Golden Gumball*!' said Cosmo, jumping down the hatch. 'I named it when I was five.'

'There are hammocks to sleep in,' Magnus called. 'Come and see.'

'The top one's mine. The top one's mine,' Gus chanted, kicking his feet off the wall and swinging his hammock backwards and forwards. 'I've already licked it so no one else will want it.'

Cosmo leapt into another hammock. 'Well, I'm having this one. It's the biggest.'

'There aren't enough hammocks for all of us *and* the animals,' said Magnus, counting quickly. 'We'll have to top and tail. Gus and Bob, Cosmo and Sid.'

'I'm not sharing with a sloth,' Cosmo interrupted. 'It's bound to snore.'

Magnus ignored him, and continued. 'Saskia and me. Esme, you and Donk can share because Freddie doesn't need one.'

'Thanks, Mags,' Esme said, flinging her

suitcase into her hammock. 'I can hear Mrs Larder calling. We'd better go and help.'

Mrs Larder was hot and flustered, herding a squawk of chickens and Ellie the cow up the plank and into a hay-filled hold on board.

'Do hurry the cow along, Mrs Larder, or you'll be coming with us,' Uncle Mac called, heaving up the sails and releasing the boom. 'We have a long journey ahead. What are you

doing down there?'

Mrs Larder bustled back out on to the deck and down the landing plank. Throwing over the landing rope, she blew kisses and shouted goodbyes before hurtling back up to the castle.

'The sail is stuck,' Cosmo called. He gave it another hard tug and leant far out over the edge of the boat with all his weight.

'Don't worry, I'll fix it!' Esme called as she leapt up the mast like a tree monkey. 'All done!' she shouted as she somersaulted back down.

The sail flew up and Cosmo, on the other end of the rope, splashed straight into the sea.

Esme peered over the edge. 'Ooops. Sorry, Cos.'

Cosmo hauled himself back on deck.

'Esmmmmmmeeeeeeeee!' he yelled, charging straight at her.

Esme back-flipped over him as he tripped and slid straight back into the water again.

'Do it again. Do it again!' shouted Gus, jumping up and down.

'You've had it now Esme,' Cosmo shouted, pulling himself out of the water for a second time. 'You had better sleep with your eyes open. I am going to find a way to get you back.'

'That's enough messing around,' Uncle Mac called. 'First of all, the rules. *One*: everyone does what I tell them. *Two*: there can only be one captain and that's me. *Three*: there is a timetable here. Never be late for duty and never miss your hammock time. Magnus and Esme, you will do the first night duty so that Magnus can teach you how to sail. Now – positions, everyone!'

Cosmo stomped around the deck, complaining about not getting to be on the first night duty.

'Please remove Sid from the mast,' Uncle Mac ordered. 'And Saskia from the boom and get Bob from under my feet.' He pointed north. 'Let's sail. To the Arctic!'

FIVE

★ ★ ★

The Great
Whale Rescue

(Part One)

The *Gumball's* sails flicked out to tickle the
wind. In a playful mood, it chased the sails
and blew them forwards, faster and faster,
until the boat became a galloping horse,
hurtling across the waves.

Clinging on with all their strength,
Magnus and Esme held the bucking boat
straight and sped for hours, their faces
glistening with sea spray and excitement

while the rest of the crew slept soundly below.

Calming the boat to a canter across the quieter waters, a little north of midnight, Esme scanned the sea restlessly, like an owl looking for prey. She was proud to be on the first night watch and didn't want to miss a moment.

'Just look at the night,' she gasped with delight. 'There are more stars than sky up there.'

Wrapped up in the twinkling darkness, Esme and Magnus watched the light from the stars dance delicately on the sea, performing for the thousands of fish below. It was quite a show.

'What's that, Magnus?' Esme asked

suddenly, peering out at the most shadowy of shadows in the night.

'I'm not sure.' Magnus followed her gaze 'Where are the binoculars?'

Esme scrabbled beneath the mounds of extra coats behind the wheel. She was too late. 'I think it's gone,' she sighed. 'Perhaps I imagined it.'

Magnus reached for the binoculars. 'No, there was definitely something.'

'I'm going up the mast to look.' Esme tossed a long rope over her shoulder and started to climb. Throwing the rope out from the top of one mast, she lassoed the other mast and pulled the rope tight. Having double-checked the knots, she tightroped to the middle for a better view.

'Can you throw up the binoculars?' she
called to Magnus.

He tossed them high. 'On their way!'

Esme caught them on her foot. 'I can
see much further from up here . . . There *is*
something there. It's another ship! Oh my
stiltwalking aunts! It has a mast and boom like
bones . . . I think I can see a skull on the sail
. . . Magnus, I think it might be a pirate ship.'

Diving down from the tightrope, Esme

somersaulted onto the
deck to look again.

'They're getting
closer,' she said desperately,
as the ghostly galleon sailed
into clear view. It towered above
them, tattered and torn.

Magnus stared up, 'It does look
sort of familiar.'

'It *is* familiar,' Esme cried. 'It's
the pirate ship from last summer. Uncle Mac
was right to worry. They must be after the
animals.'

Magnus adjusted the wheel. 'We have to
get away.' He hauled the sails in tight against
the wind, which lifted them like the wings of
a bird and flew them across the waves. Faster

and faster they glided, and larger and larger
the stretch of sea between the pirate galleon
and the little boat grew.

Esme clambered
back up to her high
wire to keep
a lookout.
'Icebergs,' she
called. 'Be careful.
We're heading
straight for one.'

'We'll have to slow down,' Magnus
decided. 'We can't steer round it at this
speed. It's too dangerous. That iceberg is
the size of a mountain, it'll smash the boat to
pieces.'

'But if we slow down, the pirate circus

will reach us and steal the animals,' Esme said desperately.

A frantic tapping started on the side of the boat. Esme looked over to see Freddie knocking with his long unicorn-like horn. 'I think Freddie wants something. Watch!'

Freddie swam around to the front of the boat and waved his head towards the ice floe.

'He wants us to follow him,' said Magnus.

'But we'll hit the ice if we go that way,' Esme called.

As they paused, the pirate ship whipped up the wind and hurtled towards them. Soon only a slither of sea separated them.

'We've got you now!' A familiar voice spat across the narrow gap. 'Hand over the animals you stole or you're going down.'

In the moonlight, the snarling features
of Ringmaster Captain Harm glowed. He had
a hook for an arm and a smile like an electric
eel. His face leered straight at Esme.

Shocked, she stumbled back off the wire,
and dived for the deck. She huddled close to
Magnus.

'What do we do?' she asked. Her voice

was so quiet that it could have been a seahorse that had spoken.

'We've got no choice, Es.' Magnus whispered back. 'They're only a leap away now. We *have* to trust Freddie.' He turned the wheel slightly towards him. 'Tighten up the sails again, we're heading straight for the iceberg.'

Hardly daring to breathe, they followed Freddie across the icy sea. Closer and closer to the ice mountain they charged, until it was all that they could see. The pirate boat breathed down their necks, so near, their vile voices echoed in Esme's ears.

The pirates hackled and cackled. 'We'll take that donkey thing too. And the sea will take the rest of you.'

With a wall of ice in front of them and a
pirate ship behind, Esme was overcome with
fear.

'This can't be right, Mags,' she said, as
Freddie swerved suddenly. He appeared to
swim straight into the ice mountain's endless
side with just a flick of his fin. Esme covered
her eyes, waiting for the shattering sounds of

wood splintering on ice as they charged on.

Without a breath, Magnus pulled the boat round to where he had last seen Freddie, and sailed blindly into a small icy opening hidden in the never-ending wall of whiteness.

'Look, Esme!' he shouted in amazement, pulling her hands from her face. The high, narrow entrance opened into a huge cavern and the boat slowed to a stand still in the centre of a windless crystal dome.

Esme peeped out slowly from between her fingers.

'Isn't it beautiful?' said Magnus.

Esme's eyes adjusted to the startling vision. The lights from the boat explored the momentous internal water walls of the glistening mountain. Ice had formed into

pillars and dripping chandeliers. It glowed
and sparkled with the moving light.

From the darkness at the end of the small
opening a dull thud sounded, followed by
splintering and shouting.

'It's the pirate ship!' Esme jumped up.
'They've crashed!'

Swimming between the pillars of their
home, a pod of Narwhals circled the boat in
celebration. They dived under and over one
another, pushing their brothers and sisters
playfully with their tails.

'Look, Freddie's found his family,' Magnus
said. 'Our first animal returned to his home.'

Esme leant as far over the edge of the
boat as she could. 'Thanks, Freddie!' she
called into the water.

'We can't stay here for long, though,'
Magnus said. 'They know we're here.'

Splashing sounds from the hidden
opening became louder and louder.

'They're swimming over to us,' Esme
yelled. 'We have to move.'

Freddie surfaced and wrapped one of

the boat's ropes around his horn. The other Narwhals copied him until there were twenty or more at the bow of the *Golden Gumball*. Pulling it hard, they guided the boat across the crystal cavern and through a tunnel at the other side.

Emerging back into the wind-whirled night, Magnus quickly captured the breeze in their sails and skipped the boat away over the star speckled sea.

Studying the moonlit map twinkling in the darkness above, he sailed them on north through the salty night towards morning.

Freddie swam away to the west as Esme waved goodbye. She watched him become a silhouette, and then a shadow, and finally, as he should always be, a part of the sea.

SIX
★ ★ ★

Donkey Sick

The startlingly white landscape of ice sculptures, framed only by the bluest sea, was enough to wake Esme immediately.

'That is completely amazing!' Esme leapt up the mast and on to the tightrope to get a better view. Thousands of years of wind and sea had chipped away at the ice, sculpting it into beautiful forms; an ice garden of statues displayed across the sea. With binoculars, she hunted behind each of the monumental

white forms to see whether the splintered
pirate ship lurked there, but it could not
have disguised its darkness in the middle of a
seascape of light.

'They must have swum back to the
ship,' Esme called to Magnus. 'I can't see it
anywhere.'

'We need to keep moving. It's not safe. I'll tell Dad about the pirates after breakfast,' Magnus replied.

Esme leapt down. 'I'm ravenous! I'll just check on Donk and then get cooking.'

'Oh, poor Donk, you really don't look well.' Esme lifted his mane to feel his head.

Stretched out with his hooves in the air, Donk lay in the hammock, looking green around the snout.

Esme leant in closer to him. 'Are you OK, Donkins?' she asked gently.

'Eeeeeeee-aawwww-owwwwwwwww,' Donk whimpered back.

'Stay in bed, Donkers. Let me tuck you in.' She sang him a lullaby and kissed his slightly green snout back to sleep. On her way out, she glanced at Cosmo with his covers pulled up to his ears in the bunk below. 'Call me if you need me, Donk,' she whispered.

Magnus sniffed out the food before it arrived. The tempting smells of crispy bacon, hot chocolate, toast, maple syrup and sausages

tiptoed out of the kitchen,
up the stairs and on to
the deck.

'Morning,
Uncle Mac,' said
Esme. She handed him a plate of buttered
toast to take up, and followed behind with
the tray.

Uncle Mac put his arm around Magnus's
shoulders. 'So how was the night watch?'

'Well . . . it was exciting . . .' said Magnus.

Uncle Mac strode over to collect a bacon
sandwich. 'Oh yes! The first night watch
is always exciting. All that fresh sea air, the
moon, the stars . . .'

'. . . the pirate ships,' said Esme.

'The inside of icebergs,' said Magnus.

'The desperate escape,' said Esme.

'Sounds as though you had an adventurous night,' said Uncle Mac.

Esme and Magnus told him the story. Woken up by the smell of sausages, Gus came up to join them just as they got to the part about Freddie and his family and how the Narwhals had rescued them.

'It is too risky for us to drop Saskia back in Siberia.' Uncle Mac pointed at the map.

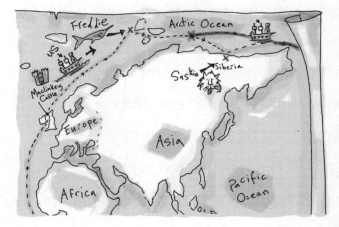

'We need to put as much sea between us and the pirate circus as we can.'

'Perhaps we should head straight to South America to take Sid back instead,' Magnus said. 'I don't think that Saskia will mind staying with us for a bit longer.'

She was curled up across his feet as a foot warmer. She hated to be far from his side and Magnus wasn't sure that she was ready for the wild just yet anyway.

Uncle Mac took another bite of his sandwich and chewed thoughtfully. 'Good idea. We'll head straight for the coast of Peru where the Amazon meets the sea. That should put them off our tail.'

'How will we get Sid back to the jungle?' asked Magnus. 'It's quite a way from the shore. If we moor up for too long we'll give the pirates more of a chance to catch up.'

'I have friends there who can take him back to the jungle,' Uncle Mac replied. 'I'll send Erica and Jim a message now. Actually, if we sail fast enough, we should make it just in time for the carnival.'

Uncle Mac whistled over the edge of the boat and a couple of migrating geese swooped down and landed next to him. He fed them the crusts of his sandwich, wrote a quick note, tied it to their necks and sent them on their way.

Singing started up over the sound of the geese's wings beating on the wind. Esme looked around and found Gus sitting on the boom with his legs hanging down, peering into the water.

'I love you little whales,
I love your squidgy backs,
You look like weird unicorns,
But your legs are a tail.
Goodbye rubbery creatures,
I know you'll be free,
But I love you a lot,
Don't forget about . . .'

'Arghhhh . . .' came a howl from below deck. 'Donkey sick! Donkey sick! Someone help. I'm covered in Donkey sick . . . get that revolting creature out of here!' Cosmo yelled from below.

'Shush, Cos. Gus is singing,' Magnus said, sticking his head down the hatch. 'What are you yelling about?'

'My hammock is swimming in donkey

sick. It's disgusting.
It smells worse than
mouldy yak's milk.
Donk's been sick all
over me. I'm going to
throw that grotesque,
mulesque thing of yours
overboard. Esme, this is
your fault yet again. You
just cause trouble all the
time.'

Cosmo clambered
up and lowered a bucket
into the sea and tipped
it over his head to wash
the sick off.

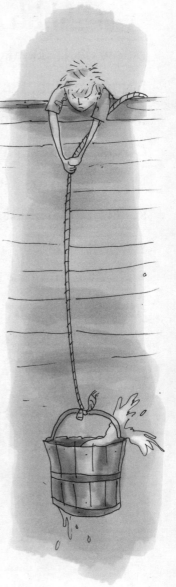

'**Arghhhh!** It's freezing,' Cosmo shrieked.

'We're in the Arctic, Cos.' Magnus tried not to laugh, as Cosmo stomped below deck for clean, dry clothes.

'I'd better go and clear up,' Esme sighed, lowering the bucket for fresh water before heading down to look after Donk.

'I'm really sorry, Cosmo,' she told him. 'I've cleaned up all of the mess from your bunk. I think that he's just a bit sea sick.'

Cosmo grunted. 'I don't care what he is. He's revolting and he doesn't belong here and neither do you.'

Esme curled up next to a cleanly wiped Donk and put her arms around his neck for comfort. 'Don't listen to him, Donk. I'm sure he doesn't mean it.' She put her face deeper into Donk's mane. 'Don't let it upset you, Donk. I think he's just still cross about the night watch.' Donk snored.

It was Esme's bunk time until lunch and she fell asleep, a little sadly, but dreaming of ice caverns and sea sculptures.

Cosmo stomped around below deck. 'I wouldn't sleep if I were you, Esme,' he thought. 'I will get you back. Just you wait. And it will be just when you are least expecting it.'

*

Esme slept like a sloth wrapped in the warmth of Donk. Magnus slept soundly in the hammock above her. Despite it being bright daylight outside, the two of them were exhausted from the adventures of the night-watch and lulled by the gentle rocking of the boat as it made its way south.

'Mags,' Esme whispered when she woke.

'Yup?' Magnus answered sleepily.

'It's Gus's birthday while we're at sea,' she said.

'It is?' Magnus replied.

'Yup and we didn't bring any presents,' Esme answered.

Magnus sat up in his bunk. 'We need to make something.'

'Let's do it now while he's on duty so it's a surprise.' Esme kissed Donk, who looked much better, and threw a couple of old jumpers on.

'I'm going to make him a whale encyclopaedia,' Magnus said, reaching the kitchen table. He scrabbled around for scraps of paper and some pens.

'We ought to tell Cosmo, so he's got time to make something,' said Esme, opening the biscuit tin.

'Good idea. We'll tell him as soon as his shift starts. I'll start with information about Narwhals.'

Esme wandered into the chicken hold and collected stray feathers. Then she cut up a really old tea towel, and made it into a cushion shape. She stitched a Narwhal on to the front, before stuffing it with feathers.

As the large sea clock struck the hour of their next shift, Esme tied a ribbon of fishing net over the old map wrapping

paper. They hid the presents underneath
Sid, and ran on deck to shouts from Uncle
Mac and Cosmo.

SEVEN
★ ★ ★

Birthdays and Banana Mousse

'Grab the ropes!' called Uncle Mac, as he threw them the mainsail. 'Cosmo has just spotted the pirate galleon again. We need all hands on deck.'

Esme and Magnus anchored the ropes and leapt to the helm. Night and day shifts blurred together as all hands were needed on deck.

Following Uncle Mac's new route, they sailed south, into torrentially rainy days and out of thunderously lightning-streaked

nights. They barely saw their bunks and being dry became only a dream. Until, at last, after two months had stormed past, the clouds finally let the sun out to play on the sea. Exhausted waves dozed into ripples and the warm water around the equator invited the children in.

Sightings of the pirate ship had disappeared around the edge of Canada several weeks before, and the crew of the *Golden Gumball* had relaxed into a holiday mood.

Steering to a sandy shore, Uncle Mac moored the boat by Peru, just in time for Gus's birthday. The children dived off the deck and chased each other under the cosy water and back out into the sunshine.

Roasted to a gentle brown with freckle-speckled cheeks, Esme, Magnus, Cosmo and Gus became giddy with warmth. They wrapped themselves in towels and told stories around a beach bonfire, late into the night.

*

'Happy Birthday to me. Happy birthday to me, happy birthday dear meeeeeeee. Happy birthday to meeeeeee!' sang Gus, as he woke everyone on the boat up early the next morning.

'Good morning. Good morning!' He jumped from hammock to hammock to wake them up. 'I said, "Happy birthday to me. Happy birthday to *me*."'

'I want to be asleep,' complained Cosmo. 'It can't be morning already.'

'It really is!' Gus pulled up the blind over the porthole and the light poured in.

'Happy birthday, Gus,' Esme said sleepily.

'Happy birthday, little broth.' Magnus ruffled Gus's hair.

'Get off me or I'll kick you,' Cosmo said, trying to shove Gus out of his bunk.

'Happy Birthday!' Uncle Mac scooped Gus up on to his shoulders and carried him out on to the sunny deck.

A loud squawking, followed by thuds from above, brought Esme, Magnus and Cosmo up behind them.

Birds circled
above, singing.
Two seagulls
had bright
envelopes
tied around their necks with red, stripy
ribbon.

Magnus whistled, and they swooped
down to perch on the wheel so that he could
untie the bows.

'Look, presents!' Esme called, admiring
the pretty packages that littered the deck.
'The birds must have dropped them for Gus.'
She scooped them up in her arms.

'What would you like for breakfast,
Gus?' asked Uncle Mac. 'Cosmo and I are on
cooking duty this morning.'

'Pancakes and maple syrup and ice cream with bananas, please,' Gus said, without needing to think.

Uncle Mac organised them. 'Es, can you fetch eggs from the chickens? Gus, I know it's your birthday, but could you milk Ellie? She'll kick anyone else who tries. And Magnus, could you lay the table?'

Magnus found the presents that they had hidden under Sid, and added them to the pile on the table.

'What are those?' Cosmo asked his brother.

'Presents for Gus,' said Magnus, pouring out the orange juice. 'Es and I made them a while—' He stopped when he saw Cosmo's face. 'I'm so sorry, Cos. We meant to tell you so that you could make something too. We completely forgot because of the pirates.'

'Thanks a lot!' Cosmo banged the frying pan down on the stove. 'It's just you and Es again, is it?' Then he had a brainwave. 'Dad, will you help me make a catapult for Gus?'

'What a great idea.' Uncle Mac cleared a space on the table and they drew out the plans. 'But now the birthday breakfast is ready!' he called, and rolled up the plan to give to Cosmo. 'I'll help you build it later.'

Gus opened the presents from his father first: his very own compass and telescope.

'Thank you, thank you!' said Gus. 'Can I sail the boat on my own now?'

'We'll see,' said Uncle Mac, laughing.

'These ones are from Mum,' Gus said, covering them all in a flurry of tissue paper as he opened the parcels the birds had dropped on deck that morning. Model aeroplanes

and working miniature trains and bags of
American sweets fell out.

My darling Little 5 year
old boy,
how time flies!
So sorry not to be with
you on your birthday
all my love is there to
keep you warm. I hope
you like your presents.
Huge hugs
Mama xxxxx

Next, he dived
into the presents
from Esme and
Magnus. 'I love
them!' After
hugging them
both, he looked
at Cosmo
expectantly.

'I'm still
building it,' Cosmo said. 'And it's
not my fault it isn't ready.'

'I'll love it anyway,' Gus said. 'Thanks,
Cosmo.' He hugged his brother, and then
picked up a large blue envelope.

'I hope this one is from Mrs Larder,' Gus

said, tearing the other card open.

Happy 5th Birthday!

To my youngest chick!
Here's the first clue to find
your birthday hamper and
presents...
    Kisses
Mrs Larder
x x x x x

Clue 1
This keeps you
floating...
(hope you haven't had
to use it yet!)

'The life jackets!' shouted Cosmo.

They found the second clue
under the life jackets.

Clue 2
Fill me with water
and find the soap.....
(you probably haven't
used this yet either,
naughty children!!)

'The bath!' they all
cried together. 'She's right.
We haven't used it yet. It was too cold to
undress in the Arctic and now it's so warm,
we wash in the sea! I'm not even sure that
I've seen it.'

'It's in the kitchen cupboard. Bob's
sleeping in it,' said Gus. He added proudly,
'He snored so I made him a bed in it. He's
got tea towels for blankets.'

'We'll bring it up on board,' said Magnus.
'Bob needs some fresh air.'

The third clue, taped to
the bottom of the bath said ...

Clue 3
In the hay where
breakfast is laid.....

'The chickens!' squawked Esme. 'It must be hidden in the hay with the chickens.'

They clambered over each other to try to get in there first, scaring the poor chickens who had to leap out of the way as Magnus, Cosmo, Gus and Esme scrabbled around in the hay.

'I've got it! I've got it! I've got it,' Gus shrieked as they all ran to help him pull it out of the piles of fresh hay.

Undoing the buckles, Gus flung open the hamper and pulled out:

♡ Your Very own
Birthday Hamper ✽
✽ ✿ Contents ✽
8 Packets of Jelly
24 Spotty balloons
Party hats
5 coloured candles
Bunting
5 presents
1 x Packet of felttips
1 x book
1 x Paints + brushes
Table cloth + sparklers
♡ Chocolate Cake Mix !!♡

The others looked at the contents of the hamper and started to plan.

'If we get Bob out of the bath, we can use it to make up all the jelly,' Esme said. 'Let's take him for a walk around the deck. He could really do with some exercise.'

Magnus coaxed Bob out with some left-over banana mousse and spread a trail around the deck so that he could eat his way round. Magnus and Esme took turns pouring lemon, cherry, orange, lime, blackcurrant, strawberry, raspberry and pineapple jellies into the bathtub and left them to set.

On each lap of the deck, Bob sniffed around the catapult.

'Get out of the way,' said Cosmo. 'Otherwise I am going to use *you* to test it.'

'Where's Sid gone?' Magnus asked. 'I don't think he's left that hammock for the whole trip, except to eat.'

'He's wrapped around the mast, fast asleep,' Cosmo replied. 'I don't know why the pirates bothered capturing him. He's the least entertaining animal I've ever seen.'

Across the deck of the boat, Bob waddled

around one final time,
licking up any bits of
mousse that he had
missed on previous
rounds.

'You have to see
what I've made for
Gus for his birthday,'
Cosmo shouted.

'What is it?' asked Esme, looking at the
strange contraption in front of her.

'It's a giant catapult,' said Cosmo. 'Do
you still not know anything?'

'It looks great,' Magnus said, pulling on
the enormous rubber band that Cosmo had
made from Donk's old unitard.

Cosmo glared at Bob. 'It's huge, big

enough to fire the pygmy hippo if we needed
to.'

'Why would you need to fire a pygmy
hippo?' asked Gus, who had just stuck his
head out to show them his chicken drawing.

'Look Gus,' said Cosmo. 'It's for you.
Your own catapult!'

'Wow, thanks, Cosmo.' Gus looked at the strange contraption and wondered what to do with it.

'Let me demonstrate how it works. Bring me some jelly,' Cosmo ordered.

He loaded up the catapult with the multicoloured jelly that Gus was bringing to him by the armful. 'Jellies away!' he yelled as he pulled back, let go, and watched the jelly shoot out to sea in a perfect rainbow.

'It's brilliant, Cosmo,' Esme said. 'Just think what else we could do!'

'No!' Cosmo said.

'Why not?' Esme asked.

'Because if we used your catapult as part of the act,' Esme said, 'you could put me and Donk in it. You could fire us up to the high

101

wire. It would be fun!' she pleaded, hopping with excitement.

'OK, maybe,' Cosmo said. 'But don't forget it's my catapult . . . well, maybe a little bit Gus's.'

Esme climbed in first to test it out before Donk. 'Please don't pull it back too far, Cosmo, or I'll end up in the sea.'

Cosmo pointed the catapult at the tightrope and pulled backwards. 'I'm going to count to three . . . one . . . two . . . three!'

The catapult leapt forwards and Esme shot through the air, somersaulted once, and landed perfectly on the middle of the tightrope.

'Again, again, again,' shouted Gus.

'Let's try Donk now,' Esme said, sliding

back down the sail. Donk looked nervous.
'It'll be OK, Donk. I promise. It's really good
fun.'

Cosmo and Esme loaded him in and
Cosmo pulled back gently under Esme's
watchful eye. Donk sailed through the sky in
a beautiful curve before tipping himself into a

spin around the high wire.

'Perfect, Donk! You brilliant creature!' Esme shouted.

'What about trying both of you together?' Cosmo suggested. 'That would look amazing.'

Esme and Donk climbed in. Cosmo pulled back and sent them flying up. Donk dipped into his spin as Esme somersaulted in midair before landing, balanced on Donk's back, in the middle of the tightrope.

'I want a go. I want a go!' Gus clambered in.

'OK. I'll just rig up that old fishing net as a safety net,' said Esme from halfway up the mast. 'Then you can land in that instead of the high wire.'

'You should all have a go,' said Uncle Mac. 'I haven't seen the things that you learnt

in the circus with Esme last summer. Put on a
show for me.'

Being catapulted was so much fun that
Bob, Saskia and Sid all wanted a go. Uncle
Mac made some hoops from old fishing wire
and hung them from the high wire for the
animals to be fired through. They landed

safely in the net each time, slid down the sails and pushed one another out of the way for their next go.

'I'll get the sparklers,' said Esme. She slid down to grab them. 'It's starting to get dark now. We can be like the flame-thrower act in the circus.'

'Then you can call your new act "Amazing Esme and the Catapulting Creatures,"' laughed Uncle Mac.

He tied the birthday bunting to the tightrope and clambered down to light the candles on the large chocolate fudge cake that had been baking below deck.

So, framed by a moody moon and decorated by mist-softened stars, they drew light on the night between mouthfuls of cake.

Blissfully unaware of the evil audience that watched from behind a jagged rock, the children performed old tricks and new, silently mocked by the pirate clowns' waiting glare.

EIGHT
★ ★ ★

Carnivals and Cutlasses

'My friends, Erica and Jim, have replied at last,' said Uncle Mac, saying goodbye to a retreating alpaca. 'They are arriving here on the shore as part of a carnival this evening. They've asked if we'll take part.'

'A real carnival?' Esme asked. 'With real costumes and music and dancing?' Esme had heard amazing stories about carnivals from the circus acts at home.

'Yes,' Uncle Mac said. 'I thought that we could all perform with them. You could do your new routine with the catapult.'

'Oh, my galloping grandfathers! That would be the most fun ever!' Esme exclaimed. 'We had better practise and make costumes and paint our faces and . . . '

'. . . keep a look out,' said Uncle Mac firmly. 'It won't be long before those pirates find us. We must set sail as soon as Sid is safe.'

*

In the early evening, the sky changed into a sunset-striped costume to join the carnival. A thousand spectacular performers dressed

as exotic birds shimmied around the corner on to the gold-glittered beach. The beating of drums from the boat mingled with carnival music and the land came alive. Esme's face could hardly hold on to her smile. She felt all the fun of the circus surround her as she climbed into the catapult with Donk to begin their new routine.

Waiting there, in a costume sewn from shells and seaweed, Esme realized the carnival was changing from being the sequinned star act into a swaying, shimmering audience . . . watching her.

Halfway through their routine amid thunderous applause, Esme glanced out to sea and gasped in horror as a bone-shaped mast sailed into view.

'The pirate ship!' she called desperately, holding Donk back from the next move. But no one could hear her above the cacophony of the carnival.

Gus saw them next as he flew out of the catapult and through the hoops.

'Real pirates!' he yelled as he landed. 'Cosmo, you lied to me.'

'Not now, Gus,' shouted Cosmo.

'But you told me pirates didn't exist.' Gus was furious. 'I thought that they were made up, like skunks.'

'Skunks aren't made up, Gus,' Cosmo shouted over the cannons and carnival music. 'Don't talk. Just move. Quickly.'

Two huge explosions and three pirate clowns were fired through the air. They hit the deck, hard. Clambering up the mast and boom, they clenched cutlasses tightly in their broken, blackened teeth.

And the chase began.

'Animals. We want animals!' snarled the largest pirate. His legs were as long as a stilt-walker's and he had arms to match. He lunged at Donk. Donk somersaulted out of reach, and he scooped the sloth up from under the boom.

Thinking quickly, he carried him safely to Erica and Jim on the shore, he said goodbye from them all. The carnival thought that it was all part of the act. They danced their applause as they shimmied off to the jungle with the sleepy sloth.

Explosion after explosion sent more clowns flying over. In a flash, five strode along the tightrope towards Esme. They grabbed at her. Pirouetting out of the way, they tumbled into the safety net. Uncle Mac and Cosmo spun them round tightly, and no amount of kicking got them out.

'Behind you, Cosmo!' yelled Esme as she helped the other animals to hide below deck.

Whipping around, Cosmo faced a hideous sight: a pirate with green-tinged skin and seaweed hair. Cosmo tripped him from the boom. The pirate flipped up into the catapult and Cosmo sent him screaming

startled screams straight back

out to sea.

More explosions

followed, and more pirate

clowns hit the deck. They

cut free

the others,

shredding the safety net.

They dived down hatches

and out through port holes,

a whirlwind of wicked

intent.

In the middle of the

storm, Uncle Mac, Magnus,

Gus and Cosmo were all tied

to the mast.

Esme and Donk were the only hope.

Captain Harm caught them both as they
ran to the rescue.

'Now I have all I need: a performing
mule and girl for my circus. You don't look so
clever now, ruining people's jobs . . . stealing
people's animals . . . eh girl?' he spat.

Tying them tightly, he frothed at the mouth with each word. 'Right, you're coming back to the pirate ship with me, my girl, you and your ugly mule.'

Captain Harm pulled the ropes behind him and dragged them down and across the deck. The pirate ship cut out the moon. Its ragged sails whipped the wind as it waited.

Esme fought against the ropes, desperate to rescue Donk. But the ropes held fast.

'Leave the other animals,' Captain Harm called. 'These two are already trained. They'll be much less trouble than those other stupid ones.'

'Back to the galleon!' the pirate clowns yelled and jumped into the catapult one at a time. An arc of somersaulting pirates

created a hideous rainbow of nastiness as
they soared across to the hovering ship.

Captain Harm hooked Esme and Donk
with his metal arm and placed them in the
catapult. Pulling back as far as he could he
cackled with pleasure at his catch.

'Chew your ropes, Donk,' Esme
whispered into his ear. 'Then get Saskia.'

Turning to the others, Captain Harm
snarled and sneered as he pulled the catapult

back a little further. 'Straight to the pirate ship with your girl and that thing,' he spat at Uncle Mac and the boys as Donk slid out of the catapult sling and down the hatch, unseen.

Out rose Saskia, moments later. She pounced from the hatch straight onto the captain's back, and knocked him to the floor. His hook slipped off the catapult as he fell, firing Esme high up into the air. They all

watched from their ropes as she rose higher and higher, span around a cloud and began to dive back towards the deck where she landed on top of Saskia who was on top of Captain Harm.

Not wanting to be left out, Bob waddled up from below deck. In a second, he recognised the man who had starved him and forced him to do tricks that hurt. He scooted across the deck on his fat little legs. He snuffled his large snout into the bath of jelly and scooped up great mouthfuls. He waddled back as fast as he could and spat it straight in the pirate captain's face.

'You're not so brave

now, are you?' shouted Esme, climbing down
from Saskia's back. 'Stealing animals and
feeding them scraps!' she fumed as the pirate
wriggled like a worm on the floor. 'What kind
of a cowardly creature would hurt an animal?'
she demanded as Donk chewed through her
ropes.

She used the ropes to tie up the pirate,
and continued, 'You're not even a *real* pirate.

Without that pirate costume, you're just a . . . clown.'

Bob turned around and pointed his bottom at the captain.

Esme finished the last knot. 'And you're not even funny.'

NINE
★ ★ ★

The Great
Whale Rescue
(Part Two)

Uncle Mac checked the bolt as he locked
Captain Harm into one of the onboard animal
houses. 'He should be OK in there for now,'
he said. 'He has food and water and hay. But
no one is safe while the other pirates are still
on the galleon.'

Captain Harm hammered hard on the
wooden door with his metal arm. The bolts
shook.

'Well done again, Esme. What a great escape. You saved us all, but most importantly, the animals are safe.' Uncle Mac put his arm around her shoulders.
'That was quick thinking. You're a clever girl. I'm very proud.'

'Hmmphh!' Cosmo snorted, kicking the mast. Anger exploded inside him like fireworks lit by a blazing bonfire of jealousy. The unspoken words fumed out of him silently: 'What did she ever do?'

'What will happen about getting Saskia and Bob home?' Magnus asked as he brought lemonade up for them.

'I don't know,' said Uncle Mac. 'It's too dangerous to take them to their natural homes while the pirate ship is still sailing.'

Magnus poured the lemonade out. 'So are they coming home with us?'

'For now. Yes.' Uncle Mac looked out to sea at the pirate ship. 'But first we need to deal with those pirate clowns so we can get home safely.'

'Why don't you fire Donk and me over there?' asked Esme, thinking about the problem. 'We can tie them up in their sleep, then sail the boat back here and tow it to the sea police station on the shore.'

'It's a good plan, Es.' Magnus patted her on the back.

'It's a good plan, Es,' Cosmo mimicked in

a nasty voice at the other end of the boat. 'I just built the catapult that's going to get her there. But there's no "clever Cosmo". Just "Good plan, Es," "Oh you're so clever, Esme," "Oh, you saved us, Essie-woo-sick."'

Cosmo fanned the flames of jealousy inside him. He thought hard, and decided to go along with the plan. Walking over to grab a glass of lemonade, he asked Uncle Mac in as normal a voice as he could manage. 'Shall I fire them over? They're the only ones who can do it. None of the rest of us can land without a safety net.'

'I don't know,' said Uncle Mac. 'It could be dangerous. I don't know what Esme's parents would think.'

'They stuck her on a tightrope when

 she was so young she could hardly walk,' said Cosmo, losing his nice voice slightly. 'I don't think that they like her very much anyway.'

Esme defended her parents. 'It wasn't like that, Cosmo. They just couldn't keep me off it. But they wouldn't mind, Uncle Mac, honestly. They'd want me to do the right thing for the animals.'

'So, shall I load them up?' Cosmo tried not to sound too eager.

'I don't think we have any other choice,' said Uncle Mac, regretfully. 'Magnus and I will go below deck and plan a route to the seashore police station.'

Esme helped Donk up and then climbed in herself. Cosmo pointed the catapult towards the pirate ship and pulled back. Hard. He remembered just how high Esme had gone when Captain Harm had fired her up into the air by accident.

He pulled back a little further. Esme was too busy thinking about tying up more pirates to notice the extra hard tug as she settled Donk for the flight.

Cosmo thought about Esme landing him in the sea at the beginning of the trip and pulled back just a little more.

Then he remembered how Esme had got to do the first night shift without him and – unable to stop himself – he took one more step back, pulling the catapult with him.

Then, suddenly remembering the donkey sick, he leant back with all his might.

'Now let's see how clever Uncle Mac thinks they are when they miss the boat and have to be rescued.'

His arms began to hurt with pulling. 'Hah! I told her I'd get her back!' he thought as he let go.

'Dive down, Donk. Dive!' Esme yelled as

terror struck her. This was the only chance they had. The wind stole the words. But Donk knew her so well he could read her face, and tipped into a dive towards the sleepless sea. They had been flung wildly over the top of the pirate galleon and way, way out to sea.

'Donk, Donk, where are you?' Esme whispered desperately into the mist. There was no sign of Donk anywhere and she could hardly breathe with fear.

The moon, in a bad mood, had tucked itself in behind the charcoal clouds. Many of the stars were too scared to shine and the wind was starting to wail.

'Eeee-awww, eeee-awwww,' came Donk's muffled cry at last.

Esme swam towards the sound. 'Donk. Donk!' she kept calling as she swam.

Donk swam hard and fast towards her, guided by her voice, until she felt the familiar comforting feel of his fur as the waves washed him against her.

'I don't know which way to swim, Donk. I can't see any land,' Esme said. 'I can't even see the boats. I'm sorry. I thought that I could rescue you but I don't know what to do.'

The sea stretched out before her in every direction.

Soothed by one another's presence, they drifted together for a while. It was eerily quiet as the mist tiptoed more closely around them. Like a burglar, it wrapped them up in darkness and tucked them out of sight.

'All I can think about is food, Donk,'
Esme said, remembering the chocolate cake
and hot chocolate from last night. 'It must
be nearly breakfast time. I need to stop
thinking about bacon sandwiches and think
of something to help.'

Donk snorted encouragingly next to her
and she patted his neck to comfort herself.

'The whales!' Esme cried suddenly. 'I'll
have to call them. I don't know what else to

do.' She stuck her face in the water '*HELP!*
HELP!' she burbled.

No sounds came back.

'*HELP! HELP!*' she burbled more
loudly.

Nothing.

Esme called for the whales until her voice
was hoarse. Donk nudged encouragingly with
his snout every now and then, and listened
out for whale sounds with his large ears.

None came

'They must be too far away to hear us,'
Esme said, but still she carried on calling until
their empty stomachs were louder than their
calls for help.

The unhelpful moon lingered behind the
mist and pretended not to see.

Completely exhausted, Esme's thoughts were awash with toast and melted butter and jam until she was weak with hunger and could barely stay afloat. Donk put a hoof behind her neck and held her head out of the water.

They stayed like that, too weak to move. Weak from hunger, weak from thirst, weak from shouting for help.

While the moon turned its back, the wind took against them too and began to roar. It whipped up the waves and blew them hard. They rushed at Esme and Donk and tumbled them apart. Water swamped over them and took them under.

Answering Esme's cries, whole pods of whales finally flocked towards them. All the sea creatures had passed on the call for help, hurrying them to the scene.

Left at the sunken galleon, right at
the underwater mountain. Under the
shipwrecked submarine, around the seaweed
fields, sea creatures had directed the
Narwhals and other whales.

They found Esme and Donk hanging
limp beneath the water. The whales scooped
them up and held them gently in their
mouths like puppies to bring them up for air.

Christmas at Maclinkey Castle

Christmas Eve greeted them as the Narwhals
towed both the boats up the loch to moor
on the jetty. Mrs Larder and the animals had
hung lanterns and fairy lights in the trees and
they glowed gently in the winter evening.
Snow had just begun to fall.

Esme's parents arrived for Christmas and
they hurried down to meet the boat and help
them back to the castle.

'Leave the pirate clowns and their mean

captain on board for the night. They don't deserve Christmas,' called Uncle Mac as they unpacked. 'We'll give them to the police tomorrow.'

Then Uncle Mac's eyes turned a little purple as he stared hard at his son. 'Cosmo, I'd like to see you in my study at the crack of crow call tomorrow morning.' In the rush to get Esme and Donk back home, all punishments had had to wait.

*

In her room at the castle, snuggled up in the mountains of duvets and devouring platefuls of cakes and scones, Esme left out the part about Cosmo as she told her parents about the great whale rescue and how pods from all over the world had heard their call for help

and come to save them.

She described how one pod had dropped her and Donk back on to Uncle Mac's boat and how another had towed the pirate boat back and how Magnus hadn't slept for nights as he'd waited for them to open their eyes and how Gus had got the animals to sleep next to them to try to warm them up again.

'Oh good, darling,' said her mother. 'I'm

so pleased that you're OK. I have important things to discuss with you.' Her mother never usually liked too much talking. 'The circus tour has been such a success that we have extended it for another year,' she continued. 'After your brave rescue, I think that it's only fair that your father and I let you and Donk perform as a proper circus act again. In fact, we want you to be the star act.'

Esme looked at Donk snuggled next to her by the fire and wondered what to do. Suddenly overcome with tiredness and an enormously full stomach, she fell asleep.

*

Before the castle cockerel had even had time to get to work, Gus leapt out of bed, ran down one set of turret stairs and up another and stuck his head around Esme's door.

'Morning!' he shouted, scampering in and clambering up onto Esme's bed with his stocking. 'Oh good, you're awake,' he added, getting in between Esme and Donk.

Esme opened her eyes reluctantly and found Magnus lighting a fresh fire in her bedroom fireplace. She closed them again as she felt the warmth from the flames reach her.

'We have to open our stockings!' Gus said leaning over to pull up her eyelids.

They spread out their stockings on the rug by her bed in front of the fire and started to unwrap the presents.

*

'Waheee! Chocolate pigs.'
'A scarf.'
'Felt-tip pens.'
'A new torch.'
'A yo yo.'
'A whistle.'
'New gloves.'
'Sugar mice.'
'A tangerine and some walnuts.'
'Water bombs.'
'A penknife'
'Socks.'

Gus had hung one of Esme's long stripy socks at the end of her bed while she was sleeping, and set out an old hat for Donk's presents.

'Donk's got a new bow tie and waistcoat,' Esme said, 'and carrot-shaped chocolates. And I've got a new practice tutu, which is great because a seal somewhere is probably wearing my old one now. *And* new pyjamas with donkeys on!'

Esme changed into them straight away. But she still had a problem. 'I don't know what to do,' she said. 'My parents have said that Donk and I can perform back at Circus Miranda, but I'm not sure that we are ready for full-time circus performing yet.'

'Hooray! Stay here!' shouted Magnus and Gus at the same time.

'I'd love to, more than anything. I love being here and it would be good to stay still for a bit,' said Esme, 'if Uncle Mac would have me. But I'm worried about Cosmo hurting Donk again.'

Gus climbed onto Esme's lap to open the rest of his presents.

'Stay,' said Magnus, again. 'It's so much more fun when you're here.'

'HAPPY CHRISTMAS! LUNCH TIME!' hollered Mrs Larder though her megaphone just as the sound of helicopter blades shook the castle turrets.

'Mum!' yelled Gus, hurling himself out of Esme's window and down the snowy slide.

Esme pulled an old jumper on over her new pyjamas and was just pulling on the

stripy sock that had held her presents when
Cosmo came back in and took her hand.

Surprised, she let him lead her up to the
top of her turret.

She looked down at the snowy lawn in
front of her. There, spelled out in the snow
by a hundred animals was the word 'SORRY'.

'What did Uncle Mac say to you?' Esme asked, not feeling at all like forgiving him. She had heard him say sorry before.

'He said that he would send me to boarding school if I ever did anything to put anyone in danger again,' Cosmo said. 'He said if it had been anyone except you, they probably wouldn't have made it.' Cosmo's eyes became a little wet as he spoke and he looked away. 'He said that he wished that I could be more like you.'

Esme thought that probably wasn't the best thing that Uncle Mac could have said and felt a tiny bit sorry for Cosmo.

'Well,' she began, 'I still don't like you very much.' She continued carefully. 'But I think that I would like to stay here for a while if Uncle Mac will let me and it would be better if we were friends.'

'LUNCHTIME FOR THE *LAST* TIME!' hollered Mrs Larder through her megaphone. 'At the table now or it's going to the warthogs.'

'So, are we agreed?' Esme asked. 'You don't go near Donk ever again and I will think about forgiving you.'

'Agreed. I really don't want to go to boarding school,' said Cosmo. 'Can we have a Christmas truce while you decide?'

'Let's take the slide down,' said Esme

'Race you!' shouted Cosmo over his shoulder as he pushed past.

My darling Boys,

Christmas made me realise how quickly you are growing up and how much I miss you all (but not the animals... really your father could have taken the guinea pigs out of my bed before expecting me to sleep in it!).

I've had an idea. I am filming in Texas next Summer. It's a wonderful part, I'm a cowgirl who saves the town from villains. I wondered whether you might like to come and stay on the ranch? Obviously, I will be tremendously busy but we would catch glimpses of each other at least. Do bring Esme!

Love you all,

Mama xxxxxx♡

Notes from my travels
Volume 37

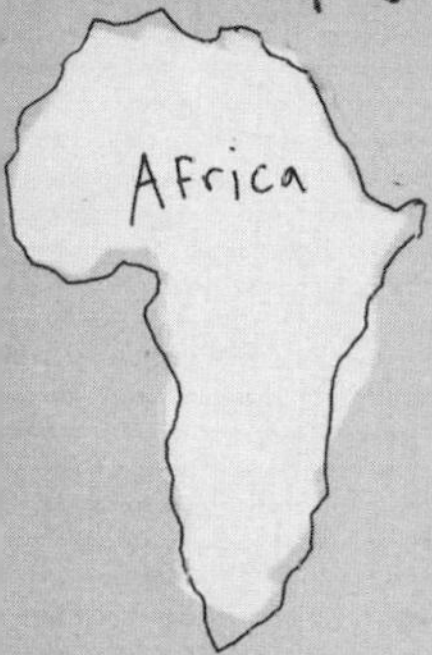

Africa

by Aubrey
MacLinkey

photographs
by Neville

5 weeks in my tree house hide
keeping a look-out for the rare
stripey tree monkey.
hmm... Looks like they found me!
thanks for telling me Neville...

We find a
friend with a
sore head.
We help him
back to health
and call him
Bertrand.

In need of HELP after walking into quicksand and no, Neville, I wasn't waving hello to you. I put the camera down and get some help you cheeky monkey!

Luckily Bertrand arrived and has a very strong trunk!

donk

flying tigers

ESme

Welcome to

make our
own
circus

Esme + Donk

ESME'S
Activity
BOOK

if you like my activity book
the sheets are available to
download online at www.amazingesme.com

not good drawing

my
best
ideas

Where in the world would
you like to go?

Can you find it on a map?

Design your own boat or Ship.

Design your own Carnival Costume

Can you draw a picture of the scariest pirate you can imagine?

Imagine you are Bob...
Write a diary entry describing
your adventures.
Write a postcard home to your
Mother in Peru.

TAMARA MACFARLANE

As a child Tamara practically lived in bookshops. She continued her love-affair with reading whilst studying English and Education, specialising in Children's Literature at university.

After a number of years spent as a literacy co-ordinator, Tamara had her first child and decided she would like to live in a children's bookshop again.

As she couldn't find one that she liked, she founded the award-winning *Tales on Moon Lane* bookshop in Herne Hill, filling it with all her favourite books.

One day, she noticed a gap in the shelves in the 5-8 year-old section and, being unable to find many books that she loved, she started to write them herself. That is when *Amazing Esme* turned up!

★ ★ ★

★ ★ ★ ★ ★ ★ ★ ★   ★ ★ ★ ★ ★ ★ ★ ★ ★

AMAZING
ESME

WELCOME
to Esme Miranda's Fairground Circus

GASP AT THE WONDROUS
UNICORNED PIG

—

Come, see the amazing
DIVING WEASLES

—

Marvel at the
PIROUETTING DONKEY

—

Laugh yourself silly at a
BAD MANNERED TEA PARTY

—

Witness a
FOOD-FLINGING EXTRAVAGANZA

★ ★ ★ ★ ★ ★ ★ ★ ★ ★ ★ ★ ★ ★ ★ ★ ★ ★ ★ ★